Usborne
Sticker Dolly Dressing
Easter Egg Hunt

Illustrated by Daniela Dogliani

Designed by Antonia Miller

Written by Fiona Watt

Contents

- 2 Painting eggs
- 4 Early morning
- 6 Easter tree
- 8 Picnic party
- 10 Baby birds
- 12 Spring meadow
- 14 Flower parade
- 16 Fairy treehouse
- 18 The Easter Bunny
- 20 Scavenger hunt
- 22 Party time
- 24 Decorating eggs
- Sticker pages

Painting eggs

Every year the dolls collect broken eggshells that have been left in birds' nests. They magically repair them, then paint the eggs with pretty patterns. When the paint is dry, they flutter away to hide them.

Willow

Early morning

If you wake very, very early on Easter morning, you might be lucky to see some fairy dolls silently hiding eggs. They search for places to put them... behind leaves, under plants and beside blossoming flowers.

Pansy

Selena

Easter tree

Every year, fairy dolls fly into treetops and tie eggs to branches with ribbons. Bees buzz around them, attracted by their shimmering wings and the sweet scent of the flowers.

Dillon

Rosina

Picnic party

In the shade of a tall tree, Sweetpea, Pippin and Petal are waiting for their fairy friends to arrive. They've prepared a special Easter picnic and have hidden lots of decorated eggs.

Sweetpea

Baby birds

Faye has spotted little birds flying in and out of a tree. Fluttering into the branches, the fairies are delighted to discover two fluffy chicks in a nest. The hungry chicks cheep and chirp while they wait for their parents to feed them.

Faye

Spring meadow

Early in the morning, you might see fairy dolls hovering over meadows filled with wild flowers and long grasses. They spread their wings to join butterflies that have come to sip sweet nectar from the flowers.

Kai

Fleur

Flower parade

Did you know that before the dolls go hunting for Easter eggs, they often take part in a flower parade? You may hear their tiny footsteps as they skip in line, carrying their flowers to their parade.

Fairy treehouse

The air is suddenly filled with a flurry of shiny wings as little dolls flutter around the branches of a tall tree. They're carrying baskets filled with eggs and flowers. Soon the tree will be decorated to surprise their woodland friends when they wake in the morning.

The Easter Bunny

Honey has spotted wet paw prints along her path. Confused by what she has seen, she called Linden and Scarlet to take a look. They think the footprints have been left by the Easter Bunny as it hopped from house to house, hiding bright eggs!

Honey

Scavenger hunt

The dolls have been given clues where Easter eggs might be hidden. As they fly over a toadstool town, they spot lots of signs. Are they clues or are they sending them in the wrong direction? Add stickers to help them.

Cosmo

Jasmin

Party time

Even though the fairy dolls are very, very tired after a busy day in Fairyland, they have a party. They play games then skip and dance, waving their arms to sprinkle magical Easter fairy dust all around.

Bluebell

Amber

Decorating eggs

Use the stickers from the sticker pages to decorate these Easter eggs with pretty patterns for the dolls to find.

Easter tree
Pages 6-7

Put Dillon's bottoms on before the top.

Dillon's boots

Rosina's clothes and headdress

Dewberry's dress and flowers for her hair

Mimosa's headdress and top

Mimosa's skirt and slippers

Picnic party
Pages 8-9

Petal's clothes

Sweetpea's blue clothes

Pippin's outfit

Baby birds
Pages 10-11

Put Lark's bottoms on before the top.

Saffron's outfit

Put Faye's skirt on before her top.

Lark's boots

Fairy treehouse
Pages 16-17

Decorate the tree with flowers, eggs, windows and doors. Add the fairies flying around.